# Who Killed Reese?

## A MURDER MYSTERY NOVELLETTE

## ASEERA

*Published by Dream Wake Work Publications @2019*

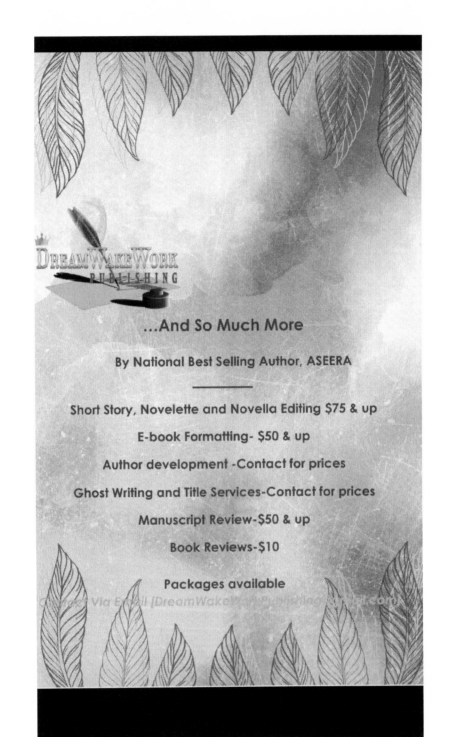

# DreamWakeWork
## PUBLISHING

## ...And So Much More

### By National Best Selling Author, ASEERA

---

Short Story, Novelette and Novella Editing $75 & up

E-book Formatting- $50 & up

Author development -Contact for prices

Ghost Writing and Title Services-Contact for prices

Manuscript Review-$50 & up

Book Reviews-$10

Packages available

Contact Via Email [DreamWakeWorkPublishing@gmail.com]

# Contents

## *Prologue*

LOOK AT THESE POSERS. I have never seen so many fake ass people together in one place. Dabbing at tears that aren't there with their expensive pocket squares and kerchiefs. Hiding their lying eyes behind their Louis and Ferragamo sunglasses. Liars the whole lot of them.

The only ones whom I could really and truly say were even remotely grieving were Franklin and Aubrey. Franklin was my on and off again boyfriend since middle school. Aubrey had been my best friend since we were five. She tried to warn me on many occasions that if I didn't stop my scheming, this may be my fate. She didn't understand that the game and all of its drama were an addiction. In the same way that people were addicted to Meth and Opioids. I needed the high of looking at the chessboard and trying to outwit my opponents, something my father taught me to play at a young age, something which I always did. I learned people didn't like losing. Yet, when up against me, they so often did.

Except for that night. I underestimated someone. It was the first time I had ever done that. I paid the price for it, the highest of prices. Now, here everyone was, saying their goodbyes. I'm never easily fooled. I think most of them were there to make sure that it was true. They needed to see the casket close on me and the dirt hit it before I was lowered into the ground. It would allow them to breathe a little easier. Or, it would help them to exhale.

At least that was what they thought. Even now, I had surprises for their asses. They would soon learn that even in death, I was not to be played with. And I loved teaching lessons.

Everyone was dressed in black. They should have been in white with purple ribbons, hats, stilettos, or scarves for my favorite color. They couldn't even respect me in death. There was one hoe there dressed in red. I expected no less from Leona. Oh, she was making a statement all right. She had reason to hate me. Reason to want to spill my blood. She wasn't one to scratch if it didn't itch. Meaning she sure wasn't going to sit around and cry for the woman who her husband was in lust with. She and I were cut from the same cloth. I knew this because I knew more about her than she thought. I always did my research. If I were going to screw you over, I was definitely going to know what made you tick.

Her ass sat next to Bucky, her husband, with a grin on her pretty face the whole time. She wouldn't even pretend to shed a tear or even sniffle. You had to admire the bitch. Really. She was really like a verse in a Jay-z song. *"Look in the casket, feeling sarcastic. Look at her, still sleeping"* No, that actually wasn't a guess or assumption. I could literally hear that song playing in her mind right now. I could hear all of their thoughts.

Taylor was one of the ones in her vintage Gloria Vanderbilt black dress and stilettos with her Christian Dior Sunglasses and matching bag pretending to cry. She had been my partner. My jealous business partner that is. I had a larger clientele than she did in the business. We had a full-service event planning and styling business.

We would style people for their events as well as arrange them. Weddings, birthdays, anniversaries, movie premieres and much more. Our company worked with wealthy clients and a few celebrities. I had started the business and brought her on later. She had good enough taste and vision, but it just wasn't on par with mine. She made decent money. I made considerably more.

When she did get big-named clients, I may have overstepped a little bit. More on that later. She was thinking that all of my clients would now come to her and she could re-imagine the business any way she liked. I had a surprise for that too.

Hugh was gorgeous. He stood at six feet even. Smooth brown skin and beautiful eyes. He had come to the viewing and not the funeral. He was a private man. On top of that. He couldn't risk being seen there at the funeral of his mistress when he was married to a high-profile talk show host. Cheyenne knew about us. There was no denying it when it broke in the blogs. Him being a football player, he was always being followed by the paparazzi. We thought we were being careful. Until a picture of us kissing at a restaurant made the rounds. Needless to say, that turned into a fiasco. Even then, he still loved me. He stayed with her because he felt he owed her for sticking by her since college. Before he made the NFL. I never asked him to leave her or pick me, just enjoyed our time together.

I could honestly say that I would miss him. And that he would miss me. We had been through something traumatic together. He was there to care for me and we helped each other weather it. He will always have a place in my heart, and I in his.

As for the rest of this lot, I should be glad to be rid of their asses. Even my mother was full of shit. She's standing there, between two ushers who are supposed to be there to catch her in case this is all too much for her. Her only daughter, gone. I watch as she tells them she will go up and say her goodbyes, alone.

Leaning into my casket, she doesn't kiss me. She whispers in my ear. *"It's about time, little bitch. I always knew this was where you would end up if you kept up your games. I could have saved myself the trouble with an abortion Thirty years ago. Rot in hell."* Well, I could feel the love from there.

She then stood up and put on a very good performance. She always was great at pretending to be a good, loving and caring mom to anyone looking in from the outside. Even though she wasn't one at all. She wailed and finally had to be helped to the back by her ushers. With a sendoff like that, you would think that she was the one who killed me. Nope, she wasn't.

I could just tell you how I ended up here, watching everyone at my own funeral, but what fun would that be? Come, let's figure it out. Who do you think did it? You wouldn't know yet. So, it's time for my confessions. Let's go.

# One

⚛

## FRANKLIN AND AUBREY

"YOU KNOW Reese would have hated this. Look at these people, here at the repass as if they are truly hurting over her. I have the mind to slap the shit out of all of them." Aubrey told Franklin in a voice that was fairly above a whisper. She had no interest in not being heard.

A few people turned their heads to look at her and whispered amongst themselves.

"Say it a little louder," Franklin told her with sarcasm.

"Do I look like I care what these people think? My friend is gone. I just can't even believe it. I keep checking my phone for another text from her." She said with tears brimming her eyes.

"Me too. A text that says something like, "Sike. I was just playing. I was running a scam." He agreed.

"I just want to know which one of these people killed her. That's what I want to know." Aubrey answered with tears flowing freely now.

Franklin grabbed her and hugged her to himself. They were a couple now. It was his job to comfort her. He had tears streaming down his face the same way she did.

"Shh. The detectives are here. They'll find out what happened that night. Lord knows they have been relentless." He reminded her.

"I hope so, but, if I find out before they do, I'm going to jail." She warned him.

"You and me both." he answered. "You and me both."

# Two

## HUGH AND REESE

"I ALWAYS HATE when I have to leave you," Hugh said as he got up and got dressed.

"Well, you know what you have to do if you want to stay." I reminded him. Talking about leaving his wife. Which, I knew was off the table. I would just mention it every now and then. Make him think it's what I wanted too. He knew better.

"I would if I didn't know how you are," he said as he pulled his shirt over his head.

I leaned up on my arm and pulled the sheet up to cover my naked breast.

"And just what does that mean?" I wanted to know.

He turned around and sat on the edge of the bed and kissed me.

"It means that you don't really want me. Not for keeps. I wish you did. If I believed that for one second, I would drop everything and run over here. You want to live your life with all that it entails."

"What does it entail? I mean, since you know everything." I challenged him. Even though he was right.

"You need excitement. You get bored easily. You don't think I know that you always have something in the works. Some plan to get

7

what you want. If you would get serious, you could have everything you wanted with me. Then again, that would be too easy. Am I wrong?" he wanted to know, leaning into me.

I kissed him and rubbed his smooth brown skin.

"Unfortunately, you aren't wrong. Yet, you keep coming back." I told him.

"Because I'm a glutton for punishment." He confessed.

"No. Because you're bored too. Cheyenne and her perfect every-thing are boring you to death. You come here for the excitement of it. If I gave everything up for you, it would be the thing"

"How's that?"

"You'd be bored here as well if I chose that path. It would be too easy for you."

"Somehow, I doubt you would bore me. It's been three years and you haven't yet." He admitted.

When he bent down to kiss me, I bit his lip gently and then stuck my tongue deep in his mouth. When I released him, he shook his head and smiled as he dabbed the dots of blood from his lip.

"See, not boring." He smiled as he stood to leave.

Just then, his phone rang. He looked down and nodded his head towards me. His way of letting me know that it was his wife. I could tell by the way she was screaming and his answers that she knew where he was. Trust and believe, she was not impressed at all.

I couldn't help but grin as I laid back down and pulled the covers over my head. He ended the call by telling her that he was on the way. Finding his way back over, he pulled the covers down and looked at me.

"Call me later?" he asked.

"I'll tell you what. Call me when you get off of punishment." I teased him.

"You think you are so funny." He jabbed, slapping my ass on the way towards the door."

"You know she will never leave you. She has an image to maintain." I reminded him.

"Oh, I know. She has made that clear. However, you, you she has it in for." He warned me.

"Tell her to get in line," I smirked.

"I will." He promised with a half-smirk that turned into a frown. I knew what he was thinking about.

It was the baby. We found out that I was pregnant a couple of months ago. It was when I was three months along. He was so happy. Two weeks later, I used the bathroom and there was nothing but blood. He rushed me to the hospital, and we found out that I had suffered a miscarriage. It was hard for us both, especially for him. He stayed by my side for weeks until I was fully cleared by the doctor.

I tried not to think about it even though it crept back in every now and then. The same for him.

"Call me." he said again as he walked out of my bedroom, not waiting on my answer. He knew I would do what I wanted and when. That included calling him or not.

# Three

## CHEYENNE

"**CALM DOWN GIRL.** I can't keep fixing your make-up before you go out on stage." My make-up artist Lex warned me.

"I don't know why you put up with his lying, cheating ass anyway. The shit is beyond ridiculous. You are the shit, pure pressure. I mean, look at yourself." My producer and best friend, Yancy told me as she sat on the edge of the couch with her clipboard.

"I love him." I damn near whined.

"Bullshit." She countered.

"What do you mean? You don't think I love my husband?" I asked her.

"That part is obvious. No, The bullshit is there is no way he canlove you the way you love him if he knows that him seeing that girl is killing you, but he keeps on going back." She explained and her logic was not flawed at all.

"What does this girl have that you don't anyway? I can't think of a thing that it could be." Lexi inquired as she worked on the stains that my tears had made through my foundation.

Holding my phone up from under the make-up apron shielding my outfit, I went to her Instagram page and pulled up some pictures

11

of her. Her skin was the perfect shade of brown. She didn't have big breasts, but they were a good enough size for her to look good in everything she had on in each picture. Her hair was different in almost every one as well. Sometimes it was pink, other times blonde. She even had blue hair and it was always flawless. Her lips were perfect. I mean, it was as if she modeled for the red KISS lips on shirts and commercials. Her eyes were amber and her stomach in perfect proportion to everything else.

There were a couple of pictures of her in evening gowns at events with a low cut back that was tight on her perfectly shaped ass. Lexi looked and said, "Oh, now I get it, she's crazy."

"Why do you say that?" I wanted to know.

"Look at her. She's always someone different. Even when she's on the beach. I mean, how many times do you change your Bikini in a day? Well, with her, apparently at least twice. Once for the pics in the sand and again for the ones on yacht." She pointed out. You could tell it was the same day because of the people in the background and her hair and nail colors weren't changed. They matched her swim-suits, too, by the way.

"So, you mean she keeps his cheating ass guessing?" Yancy asked Lexi as she looked over my shoulder at the pictures.

"Yes. That's exactly what I mean. Her body is almost identical to yours. You are also gorgeous. I hate even putting make-up on your perfect caramel-colored skin. I mean, you could do commercials for Blemish be gone or something. Your eyes are slanted and your lashes long. It's not the looks honey. I guarantee you that." She assured me.

"Yeah, it's worse if I'm listening to you. It's the fact I'm boring him to tears." I surmised from her speech.

"No, not boring..."

"Regimented." Yancy threw in there, which didn't make it any better.

"A fancy word for boring," I answered looking at her with the stank eye. "I can't help it. It's how I was raised. My parents, well, you know them. It was always about appearances. I had to be perfect all the time. I can't just become footloose and fancy-free all of a sudden. Also, he knew me for years before he married me. If he didn't like how I was, why propose to me?"

"He loves how you are. It just seems he likes how she is too. I don't see him stopping as long as she is willing to make herself available to him." Yancy threw over her shoulder as she poured me a glass of champagne that I always had before I went on stage to calm my nerves.

"Which she is. Remember, I had a run-in with her at that boutique. She basically laughed at me. Letting me know that as long as he came calling, she would answer. Bought her five-hundred-dollar sunglasses and left me standing there looking stupid." I recalled.

"She would have left me standing in a police line-up after I dragged her ass. That's just me, though." Yancy added as she sipped from the same glass of champagne she had poured for me.

Lexi laughed. I didn't find it funny. I found it becoming more and more of an option. If he wouldn't leave her alone, and she was not willing to walk away, there was only one thing that could be done. I couldn't believe I was even considering this. However, I would do anything to save my marriage. Especially now that I was pregnant.

No one knew, not even him. I was very early and afraid. We had lost two babies in the womb and I didn't want to say anything until I was a little further along. I had no intention of allowing him to leave us. It seemed that drastic measures were in order and if there was one thing I loved, it was order.

# *Four*

### TAYLOR AND REESE

"YOU CONNIVING ASS, disloyal, backstabbing ass bitch!" I yelled as I walked into our office.

Both of our secretaries and our interns looked at each other, stopped what they were doing, and got up to leave.

"No. You can stay." Reese told them. "This won't take long."

"Fine, they can stay. Fuck it. You know how hard I worked to get Eliza DuGard on my roster of stars to style. Then you come and snatch her right from under me. How could you? We were supposed to be friends." I yelled with tears falling.

Eliza DuGard was one of the hottest actresses right now. She was in almost every damn movie that was out and she was good. The best thing about her is that she wasn't a size two. She was a real damn woman with curves. Those were my specialty. She was referred to me by another actress. When I got the call, I almost choked on the salad that I was eating.

Reese even celebrated with me. Usually, she was the one who pulled the big money. The clients with names and money. I was usually saddled with the up-and-comers. Which I was okay with, too.

Money was money. To work with an A-list actress was on another level, so for me, this was my big break, so to speak.

I just received another call on my way to the office today. It was her assistant saying that Reese was going to style her for the MET Gala, not me. I knew right then that she must have gone behind my back and done something to poach her from me.

"Why did I just receive a call from Eliza's people saying that she is going to have you style her for the MET and her next three events after that?" I questioned as I threw my Christian Siriano Clutch on her desk, causing whatever papers she was working on to fly around. The bitch just smiled.

"Cute clutch, girl. Anyway," she started as she began to gather the papers back up, "I received a call from them saying that they saw what I did for Oray Kim. They inquired if I was available and it just happens that I am." She shrugged as if it was no big damn deal.

"But you knew I was supposed to be dressing her. You knew that. You knew how excited I was to finally have someone of her caliber to work with. It could have been my big break. My foot into the A-list." I damn near pleaded.

"Did you have them sign a contract?" she said as she began to type away on her phone answering emails as if this wasn't important. I snatched the damn phone out of her hand and leaned over her desk. It was taking everything in me not to slap the shit out of her.

"You know I didn't," I answered through clenched teeth.

"Then that's on you. If they come to me, and they don't have a contract with anyone else, why would I turn down good money and exposure? Do I strike you as stupid?" she threw out, leaning back in her chair and flipping her long, blonde bundles to the side.

"What do you mean why would you turn it down? Because we are friends and you knew she was mine."

"Oh, honey. That's where you are wrong. Thinking we were friends. We are business partners and no client is yours until you get that John or Jane Hancock on the dotted line. Which I did." she

16

damn near sang, waving the contract she had signed with Eliza in my face.

I snatched that shit and tore it to shreds and threw it up in the air causing Reese to just laugh again.

"Thank Goodness it was a Docu-Sign and I can print off another one."

"You are a cold-hearted bitch. It's my fault though. I saw all of the dirt that you did to other people and I continued to ride with you. I always thought that you wouldn't do it to me. We travel together, laugh together, we've even double-dated and everything else that I would do with a friend. I see now you are not in it for anyone but yourself. I see that shit clearly now." I told her sneaky ass through my gritted teeth.

"Some lessons are learned the hard way, she said as she shrugged, stood up, and snatched her phone back out of my hand.

"I quit. This partnership is over. I am taking my clients and starting my own business." I snapped back at her.

"I think that's a very bold move. We need more black-owned businesses. Especially owned by women. The problem with your plan is, well, your clients basically belong to me. So, you can take you, your secretary, and that old ass laptop, but everything, and everyone else, stays with me." She explained.

"What the hell are you talking about, Reese?" My head was spinning by this point.

"For goodness sake. Not only do you not have your soon-to-be clients sign contracts, it's obvious that you don't read them either. You can leave with what you brought. Anything that was acquired while you were here stays for a period of seven years." Was the short answer.

"Are you shitting me?!"

"Afraid not. You can take your copy to a lawyer. They'll tell you the same thing. Now, I am not telling you that you must go. You can stay here with us and continue to style the clients that you have acquired under this company until your heart is content. If you should choose to leave, which is always an option, it won't be with any of them on your client list."

My shoulders dropped in utter defeat. She had trapped me and she was right. I was just so damn happy that I was getting a chance to do what I loved, I signed the contract without reading it or having a lawyer look it over. I didn't have anyone to blame but myself. Now, I could stay here and work with this disloyal wench or leave and try to start from scratch. Who even knew what the hell she would tell people to keep me from success if I did decide to leave? She and this job were my only references in the industry and it wasn't an easy one to break into.

She stood up, grabbed some papers off the printer, slid her stilettos back on as we always walked around on the plush carpet in bare feet or slippers while in the office, and grabbed her bag and jacket.

"Well. I have a meeting. We can talk more about this later. I really do hope you stay though. I like you." she tossed out, stopping to put her hand on my shoulder. She must be a sociopath.

As I watched her go, I wondered how I could get up from under her thumb. I also hoped she would get hit by a car. I immediately felt bad for thinking that. Until I started to wonder, what did the contract say about her dying? Would the company come to me? I waited until she got on the elevator and then went into my cubicle and grabbed a copy of my contract from my bottom drawer where I kept important papers. I started to read every last word of it. There may be a way out after all.

# Five

## MOTHER AND REESE

"WHY AM I HERE AGAIN?" I asked my mother as I sat across the table from her in her kitchen. It was actually my kitchen. More on that later. She was an older version of me by only fifteen years. She could still turn heads, that was for sure.

"I wanted to tell you that your stepfather is coming home soon." She answered smoothly as she stirred her cup of tea.

I almost threw up. I couldn't believe that they were letting his ass out. More importantly, she sounded as if she were taking him back. If she had even left him at all.

"Coming home? Meaning here? To live with you?" I asked just to be sure.

"Yup. That's the plan."

I sat there and just looked at her with flames shooting from my eyes. After what he had done, I couldn't believe she had stood by him and was allowing him back into her home.

"Don't look at me like that. If I forgave you, I could forgive him too." She told me, lifting the mug of hot liquid to her lips. For just an instant, I contemplated slapping the bottom of it and watching her face burn.

"Forgive me? Are you serious? What the hell did I do wrong that I needed to be forgiven for?" I asked her in shock.

"For sleeping with my husband, that's what. I saw the way your little hot ass would walk around here. He's only a man. Of course, he would make the mistake of having an affair with a younger woman."

I could not believe that she was saying this shit with a straight damn face. I felt it was only right that I give her the facts since she was apparently trying to re-write history.

"Okay. Let's be clear. I was twelve years old the first time he touched me. He threatened to kill you and grandma if I told anyone. I was thirteen when he first full-out raped me. Same threat then as well. Fifteen when I became pregnant with his child that you forced me to give up for adoption. Although not before I pushed for a DNA test, which, btw is the only reason that sick son-of -a- bitch finally had to admit to what he had done. As far as I'm concerned, his plea deal was bullshit. He should have done life. Now, you sit here and tell me that I was flirting with his old dirty ass and brought it on myself." I huffed.

"Yes, it's exactly what I'm saying, because you did. Walking around in shorts and little shirts." She returned.

"You bought my damn clothes. And, for your information, it doesn't matter if I was walking around naked, I was a CHILD!!!" I screamed.

"Yeah, whatever you have to tell yourself." She spat out as if I wasn't making any sense.

"You know what, there is no use in arguing with you. Grandma was right. I'm glad she took me in during the trial and after. She said that you have always been jealous of me. Maybe because I look like you, but better. Who knows? I wouldn't be shocked to find out that you knew about what he was doing and allowed it so that he would stay. Either that or because you wanted to ruin me. Well, congratula-tions. You and that sick pervert did a number on me. I don't trust a soul and there is a twenty-pound bag of ice where my heart should

be." I told her. No, warned her was a better word for it. She was definitely never in my good graces and the little bit of kindness I offered
her because we shared blood and the love I had for my recently
deceased grandmother was about to evaporate.

"You've always been a selfish little bitch."

"Yeah, so you say. I guess you would know since I did come from
you." I stood up, took my tea to the sink, dumped it out and watched
as it went down the drain. I turned and leaned against the sink so that
I could say my peace before I left. She was making me physically ill.
"Listen, if you like pedophiles, well, that's your deal. Have fun. Let
me tell you this, though, the day he arrives back here with his shit tied
to a stick is the day I stop paying your bills. I can't for the life of me
figure out why I do it anyway. It's not like you were ever a mother to
me. Another thing I probably need counseling for, but who has the
damn time? I'd be there on a therapist couch for a year straight just
talking about you. I'm letting you know this, you do have a choice.
He can stay here, but I hope he's been saving his commissary, or
you've been dusting off your typing skills. Because one of ya'll asses
will be paying for your new life together. Now, if you don't mind,
hell, even if you do, I need to go throw-up in your rose bushes from
this sick shit and then head on over to a meeting. Ciao."

The look on her face was priceless. Her mouth was hanging open
and I knew I had just pissed her off. Good. She needed to know, I
wasn't funding her fuckery with the man who took my innocence
and any chance I had at a happy life. They could rot in a tent on skid
row together for all I cared. I actually hoped they did.

# Six

## MOTHER

**THAT LITTLE BIIIITCH.** I had no doubt that she would do exactly what she said. When my mother died, she left both houses to her. The one that I had lived in since my childhood, and the one that my mother had moved to when I was older and she wanted something with less bedrooms and no steps.

She had also left Reese a million-dollar life insurance policy. To me, she left shit. My mother and I never got along. Not really. Reese took pity on my ass and gave me fifty thousand. The rest she invested and used to start her businesses. She was always smarter than me, too. Especially with things like that. Even went to college. I blew through that trying to get my husband out of jail and take care of him while he was in there. I know what he did to my only child was wrong, but she was always a fresh pot. Tooting up her little lips and butt.

The truth was, I was jealous of her. Jealous of my own child. Even though I look great, especially for someone who is forty. Damn it okay, Forty plus five, she always looked better. Her body always looked just a little better. Her breast and ass, just a little bigger. Her waist just a little smaller. Her eyes, a little more intense. The second she was born, all of the attention was then on her and I resented her for it.

I always loved attention. Attention from wherever I could get it. That's how I became pregnant with her. Her father even loved her more than he loved me. He was shot and killed in a robbery when she was ten. Two months later, I was engaged to my husband and he moved in.

People might argue that I moved too fast and that what happened to her was on my lap. I say that those people can go to hell. I only told her that he was getting out so that she didn't come over unannounced like she does sometimes to check on the house. Trying to make sure that it's still up to par. Of course, it is. Not a thing out of place. Same with she and I. We always came correct with our hair, clothing and everything else. That, she got from me. There was no question that this house would be the same.

But now, if I take him back in here, she will stop paying my bills. Now what am I supposed to do? I won't choose her over him. I just won't. I am not trying to be old and lonely. The thought crossed my mind to burn the house down, but the insurance money would go to her.

I needed to figure something out and quick. The only thing I knew for sure is that I was her mother and she's not married, so if she dies...*No, Stop. Don't think like that. Don't even let it cross your mind that all of her money and businesses would come to you making you and your man millionaires. Put it out of your mind. She's your daughter for goodness sake. She's your daughter..she's your daughter....*

## Seven

## LEONA AND THE DETECTIVES

"**WELL MRS. HUBERT,** we want to thank you for coming in today. Also, I want you to know that you can leave at any time. We would, however, appreciate your cooperation." Detective Gallagher said to me. He was a cutie to be Caucasian. Those grey eyes and red hair fit him. Maybe I would slide him my personal cell number on the way out. Get a taste of that Vanilla.

"Oh, no problem. I have nothing to hide." I told him, crossing my legs so that my foot was between his open legs. This made him blush. I had on a short skirt and my legs were killer. No pun intended.

He cleared his throat and continued. His partner, Detective old man, or Jimison, was looking through some papers in a file. I watched the Confession tapes on Netflix. If he thought he was going to get some confession by playing bad cop, he had the wrong one. He started to speak first.

"Leona. May I call you Leona?" Jimison asked.

"Sure can, it's my name. Call me anything but guilty." I said with my full lips spread over my white teeth in a smile.

"Well, thank you. You know that we have been investigating the death of a Ms. Reese Young."

"Yes. Sad what happened to the little homewrecker isn't it?"

"So, you admit that you and she had issues?" he asked me, closing the file and leaning in on the table towards me. I smiled at the young one and then turned to Jimison.

"Issues? If you mean was she sleeping with my husband, then yes, she was. If you want to know if I was happy about it, then the obvious answer is hell no." I told him.

"It says in my file that you two got into an altercation a month or so back. Is that correct?"

"If by altercation you mean I caught her coming out of a hotel, wrapped around my husband like a snake, then I slapped her ass into the next week, then yes. We had an altercation. Before you open that file back up and waste your time, Yes, I beat the hell out of her car with my son's baseball bat and then keyed "whore" into the hood. I confessed.

"Well. Okay then." He nodded, seeming like he was surprised to hear me tell everything. "We want to know where you were on the night that she was killed." He asked.

"I was on a girl's trip with two of my sisters and my best friend to wine country the day her ass was killed. It came with a tour and it's all on my credit card. I decided I needed some time away from my husband when I found out about the two of them."

"I guess it's safe to say that you weren't happy to find out they were having an affair?" This question came from detective cutie. It was such a simple question, which I had already answered that it almost made me wonder about his ass. Didn't stop me from flirting, though.

"Let me ask you something, Brett. That's your name, right?" I asked, reaching over and running my finger across the nameplate he had with his name and detective number.

"Sure, you can call me Brett." He gave back along with a smile.

"If you caught your pretty little wife coming out of the hotel with another man looking more than satisfied, would you be happy?"

"No, I guess I wouldn't," he answered.

"Would you kill the homewrecker?"

"I may want to, but, no. I wouldn't." he answered.

"Then you and I are more alike than you may think. I wanted to ring her pretty little neck. After giving it a bit more thought, I decided that prison wasn't for me. I like options with my colors of clothing. On top of that, sharing a room with a woman named Big Bertha just isn't all that appealing to me. Now, if they allowed private cells with an en suite I may have considered it. They would also have to throw in the ability to leave the grounds whenever we wanted to and name brand shoes and outfits with an on-call hairdresser to style these bundles, then I may very well have been your person. They don't offer that, do they?" I asked.

They both laughed before Jimison assured me that all of that was out of the question.

"Then, I am not your person. I'm sorry. One the other hand, I won't lie and say that I shed a tear over her demise either." I told them honestly.

"Well. I think that's it for now. Can we contact you if we have any further questions?" Brett asked.

"YOU, can contact me anytime. Day or night. However, I'm afraid I do have to go. Babygirl has her first dance recital and my husband is in another room here, I assume he's answering the same type of questions. Let me save you guys some time, he's too much of a softy to kill anyone. I can promise you that." I told them as I stood and grabbed my phone and purse.

"Well, we appreciate your cooperation." Jimison let me know as I walked towards the door.

"Anytime." I told him as I winked at Brett. Yeah, I would get with him later. If my husband could cheat, what the hell. What's good for the goose and all of that.

I will admit that what hurt more than him cheating with her, was the fact that my husband seemed to be mourning her ass. I swear, if he puts on one more black shirt and just stares at his dinner that I slave hard over, it's gonna be another murder. I can promise you that.

# Eight

## REESE

I SAT on the balcony of my penthouse apartment, propped my feet up on my cushioned footstool and took a sip of wine. It was eight o'clock and I had a long damn day. I knew what would make me feel better. My own little secret. Grabbing my phone, I dialed the number.

"Hello.." The voice answered.

"Hey, how have you been?" I asked.

"I'm good. I was waiting for you to call. It's been three days."

"I know, baby. It's been a very busy week." I tried to explain.

"I thought you had forgotten about me." The voice almost whined.

"Oh, baby. I could never do that. Ever." I promised.

"Okay. Just checking." The voice snapped back with a laugh.

"You and I are just alike," I said with a smile. "So, I have good news. Actually, It's great news."

"What is it? You know I love surprises."

"This week has been so busy because I found three department stores to carry our clothing line." I explained with excitement.

"No." the voice said as it tried to hide a smile.

"Yes."

"OMG! AHHHHHH!" the voice screeched in my ear. I had to take the phone away from my so that I could keep my hearing. I was so happy to hear how happy they were.

"Now, your name is on the business as well. My lawyer saw to it. Not to mention it's in the actual name of our brand."

"Latoya Reese." The voice answered.

"That's right. Now, have you been working on any new designs?"

"Yes. I'm working on one right now."

"Great. When it's done, send it to me. Just like the others. I'll add my touch and we'll either add it to one of the collections or start a new one. How does that sound?"

"It sounds great. I can't believe that we really have our line in stores. I'm so excited. I want to tell everyone!"

"I know you do, but you have to wait. We'll throw a big party where we'll have some of the clothes there for people to see and pre-order. So, we have to keep it together. You understand me?" I asked.

"Yes, mom. I understand." She promised, a bit disappointed that she couldn't tell anyone, but still excited about what was happening for us.

"Alright. Good. I'll let you get back to your sketching, only for fifteen more minutes, Toya. Then it's time for bed, Okay?

"Yes, ma'am." She promised.

"Okay. I love you and you know you can call me anytime and tell me anything." I reminded her.

"I know. I love you too. Goodnight."

"Goodnight, baby."

I hung up the phone and just smiled. She was my life. Yes, she was born under the worse ofcircumstances. The husband of my mother had raped and gotten me pregnant. My mother forced me to give her up and thought it was a closed adoption. She didn't know that my grandmother and I had made it so that it was open. That way, when the both of us were ready, I could be in her life.

I always knew I would want to be, I just had to be stable first. Youth and instability didn't stop me from building a relationship with her. At first, I would just have them send me pictures. I was ashamed of giving her up but I was also a teen who didn't have shit. I had to start realizing how to make money and my own way in the world. When she was four, I became more involved. Visiting her once a week, but never telling her exactly who I was. The couple that adopted her were awesome and they treated her amazingly.

When we did sit her down and tell her the truth, she took it well. She threw herself in my arms and said she understood why I didn't say anything before and that she had a feeling. Especially since she noticed she and I looked alike. Something that she didn't have in common with her adoptive parents.

Latoya was so talented and had been an artist from birth, just like I was. I started a clothing line in her name and we began to sketch together. The three of us also kept her busy so she wouldn't get in trouble. She was on the swim team at school, took dance classes and piano as well. Her days were filled up and she loved it all. I was so proud of her. She was the only light in my life and the only person I loved. I could say that honestly.

My phone rang back, and I answered it without looking. I was thinking it was my daughter wanting to tell me something she had forgotten. The voice on the other end wasn't one that belonged to anyone who loved me.

"You a dead bitch. Watch your back and your front." The voice warned before hanging up.

It scared me so bad; I stood up and looked around. I didn't see anything that looked suspicious. It took me a moment to calm down. Whoever this was would have to get in line. I had a lot of enemies. Some I deserved; some were just jealous.

I stood up, looked around my penthouse and made sure everything was locked up and my alarm was turned on. Tired, I headed back to my master bedroom. I reached in my bedside table and pulled my pearl-handled gun out and checked that it was ready to go. It was. That made me feel better.

I laid down for a moment and told myself that it was probably just someone trying to scare me. I finished off my drink, took a shower and got in the bed, putting it out of my mind. The next morning. I learned better.

Dressed in a fitted pants suit with heels to match, I went down to the garage and got into my two-door cherry red Benz. I was driving along and jamming to my strong girl's playlist. As I came up to a stop sign, I went to hit my brakes and my foot went clear down to the floor. I kept trying to break but couldn't.

Screaming out, I continued to try and stop the car. I knew that I was coming up on a steep ass hill. If I started down there, I was for sure going to die and probably take some other people with me. I began to lay on my horn to warn people to get out of my way. I was also screaming out the window that I didn't have any brakes.

People were jumping out of my way and pulling over. It then dawned on me something my daddy told me before he died. He used to work on cars and was teaching me about them before the robbery that took him. I lifted my foot and pushed on the emergency brake, at the same time I pulled the gearshift to park. It brought the car to an abrupt stop, throwing me forward damn near into the windshield. Thank God for seatbelts. Shaking, I put my head on the steering wheel and thanked God and my dad.

I had the car towed to the garage that was owned by a friend and waited there for them to tell me what happened.

"Reese." My friend called my name. "Come with me."

Following him into his office, he closed the door behind me and I sat down.

"What's up. What's wrong with my car?" I asked him.

"What's wrong is that someone tried to kill you." He told me without holding back.

"What are you talking about?"

"Your brake line was cut clear through. This was intentional." He explained. I fell back against the chair with my hand over my mouth. "Who would want to kill you, Reese?"

So many names and things that I had done started to swirl around in my head. I became sick in his wastebasket before I could answer. He got me a cold water, made sure I had a rental and got to work on my car. I was too shaken up to drive so he had one of his drivers who picked customers up in vans to come and pick their vehicles up, drive the car. I had him take me straight over to my lawyer's office.

Between the phone call and the brakes being cut, someone was real life trying to kill me. I had to make sure some things were in place just in case they succeeded.

# Nine

### BUCKY AND REESE

"I CAME AS SOON as I heard." I told Reese the moment she opened her door. Stepping in, I began hugging her close to my body.

"Can you believe that shit? Someone legit tried to take me out,"

It was obvious she was shaken up. I had never seen her on edge before and I didn't like it. I wanted her to always feel safe. She felt safe with me, which is why she called.

"Come here," I told her. Taking her by the hand and leading her to the couch. I sat down and brought her to my lap where she curled up on me. Leaning her head between my face and shoulder, her breath on my neck always did something to me. I wrapped her tightly in my arms and rubbed her back and legs. "We need to get you some security," I told her.

She shook her head no. I could feel it moving back and forth.

"Why not?" I wanted to know, lifting her head so that we were looking face to face, she leaned down and kissed me. Once she pulled back, she answered my question.

"I don't want to draw attention or let this person know that they got to me."

"You're worried about how you'll look? You'll look alive. I for one would like for you to stay that way." I argued.

She just smiled at me. "Buck. I don't think anyone has loved me like you have since my daddy was alive." She told me.

She was actually scaring me that she was being so vulnerable. Her opening up like this was never something that she did and she was right. I did love her. I kissed her, hard and long. Her lips always tasted like vanilla, always. I mean, was she made from frosting?

"You're right. I do love you. I wish you would just let me be with you. I promise that I would never hurt you. You know me, you know I wouldn't." I told her.

"I know you wouldn't. It's me that would hurt you. My heart just isn't ready to love you the way you deserve. That's why I tell you all the time, stay with Leona." She confessed.

Before I could argue, she was kissing me the same way I had just done her. I stood up, her still in my arms and carried her to her room. The place where we tore the clothes from each other's bodies. I laid her down and kissed from her eyelids to her thighs. Her soft moans turned me on more than I ever had been.

I spread her legs and went to work on her sweet center, sucking her clit like it was a watermelon Charms blow pop and I wanted the gum in the center. Except what I wanted from her was her liquid explosion. She didn't disappoint. Reese released on my face and the sheets as I licked my lips to savor the taste.

Pulling me up so that I was facing her, she began to kiss my face all over. She wrapped her legs around me and I entered her. As soon as I felt her warm, tight and soft treasure, I called out. We made love for over an hour. Both having orgasms repeatedly until we both fell asleep.

Usually, I would get up and leave in the middle of the night. Leona, my wife, knew about us now meaning there was no need to rush off. She knew where I was and I wasn't all that sure that she really cared. Reese also wasn't one to allow someone to spend the night with her. This time, she didn't wake me. She just slept with her head on my shoulder, her arm across my stomach, and her leg laced through mine. My arms around her, I relaxed, smiled, and went to bed, happy.

# *Ten*

## REESE, FRANKLIN AND AUBREY

"YOU SHOULD COME and stay with me." Franklin offered.

"Uh, that would be a no. Thank you for the offer. I'll be fine."

"Someone cut your brake line, then there are the phone calls." He reminded me.

"I know. The thing is, if I start to show that I'm afraid, they will just get braver. I have some things in the works. I'll be protected." I told him.

He reached over and rubbed my hand that rested on the table. We hadn't been together in a long time, but I knew that Franklin still loved me. He would do anything for me and he did. Even though he and Aubrey were now dating. She came to me and asked for my blessing. I gave it to her willingly. If she wanted my leftovers that were still burning for me, then it was on her. Aubrey was unusually quiet at this weekly meet-up.

"What's up with you?" I asked her.

"Nothing. I mean, I'm worried for you. I just wish you would let us help you." she answered.

"You are. All of this is helping. It really is."

'If you say so." she answered, then sipped on her water.

"Let's talk about something else. Did I tell you guys that the Latoya Reese collection has been picked up at three different department stores?" I sprung on them.

"No way. That's what's up." Franklin responded, excitedly. He then leaned over and kissed my cheek. I could tell that Aubrey's smile was forced. I didn't address it though.

Aubrey had been trying to get her shoe and bag line off the ground for two years now. I would, on occasion, use one of her bags or a pair of her shoes when styling a client. The truth was that a lot of her designs were old looking. And I don't mean in a good, vintage way either.

I tried to help her a couple of times, but she got offended. I took the hint and now I don't even bother. When she wants my help, she'll ask for it.

"That's amazing girl. Everything is happening for you just the way you always said it would."

"It is and feels good, too, knowing that my hard work is paying off," I confessed.

"Yeah, your scheming too." She mumbled under her voice as she dipped her mozzarella stick in some marinara sauce and put it in her mouth.

"Aubrey..." Franklin said, calling her out.

"What?' she answered as if she didn't know what he wanted with her.

"It's all good Franklin. She is apparently in one of her moods. I love her anyway. In any case, I have to go."

"No, don't leave. Where are you going?" he wanted to know.

"I have to meet a client at the office."

"This late?" Aubrey wondered out loud with suspicion on her face.

"Yep. It's the only time she could get away."

I stood up, hugged them both, then left. I was meeting someone alright. I was having cameras installed in the office, my cars, and my homes. My tail was more afraid than I was letting on. I had also hired someone to look out for my daughter. Even though no one knew about her and I being in each other's lives but Franklin, I needed to make sure that she was safe. Just in case whoever wanted me dead had been following me.

They would have seen me at recitals, swim meets and her coming over to spend the weekends a couple of times a month. Those were the times that I went dark. No social media, work and I barely answered my phone. Sometimes, we would hop on a flight. I had even taken her to Paris for a fashion show last summer. We did New York fashion week two years in a row as well.

Someone who knew where my car was parked might know that. I may gamble with my life, but when it came to that little girl, no dice. Once the cameras were all installed, I headed home cause I was beat. The cameras had been installed there the day before. I was careful not to tell anyone that I had these systems put in place for security. I honestly didn't know who I could trust, besides Franklin and Aubrey. I just wanted to shower and go to bed. I didn't realize it would be my last night alive. Nor who it would be that took my life from me.

# *Eleven*

❧

## MY KILLER AND I

I STEPPED out of the shower and had a surprise sitting on my bed waiting for me. She had a spare key in case she ever needed to come in. I didn't expect to see her there tonight. Especially dressed like she was headed to work out. She and Franklin only lived three blocks away and we all went to the same gym which was between our homes.

"Aubs, you scared me. What are you doing here?" I asked her as I dried off and slid my robe on as I allowed my towel to drop to the floor.

She just sat there staring at me. Her eyes and face looked different. I couldn't place it, but I knew she wasn't happy.

"Why do you always have to have everything and everyone?" she wanted to know.

I had been rubbing my Vanilla bean-flavored and scented whipped lotion into my body from Dream and Design when I heard her say that. What she asked took me off guard for a moment.

"What are you talking about?" I tossed back at her.

"Money, success, men, even if they belong to someone else, you have to have it. Don't you?" she seethed.

43

"I work for everything that I have. You know that."

"I know that you scheme and connive. You add clauses into contracts, and steal clients. Whatever you have to do to get ahead."

"Work is work," I answered, shrugging my shoulders.

"Deceit is Deceit." She told me.

"I never deceived you, so why are you so mad about what I do to other people."

"Because, if you do it to them, you will do it to me." Was her reasoning.

"Aubrey. Let's be real, sweetie. You don't have shit that I want." I giggled a bit.

Her shoulders sagged and she looked away, trying to hide her tears.

"Wow. You really are a heartless bitch. I work so hard and get nowhere. Then, I'm forced to watch you prosper. I just can't do that anymore. And I do have something, Franklin."

"Girl. No one wants Franklin." I let her know.

"You may not want him, but you keep him wanting you. Calling him to help move shit. Sending him good morning text and smiley faces with hearts."

"We're friends."

"Don't lie to me. You love the fact that he is still in love with you. You play on it. Even though you know how I feel about him. I can't even watch it anymore."

"You can't watch what?" I asked her, truly confused.

"I can't watch you win anymore. It's fucking hurtful and exhausting. Especially knowing that you don't deserve it."

"*You* have been jealous of me for years. Let's be real. *Your* shit isn't taking off because *your* designs are ugly. Franklin will never love *you* the way he loves me because he's settling for *you*. Yes, I do keep him on a string. *You* have always known it yet are the one who decided to still go after him. If he's only capable of giving *you* half of his heart, well that's *your* fault for accepting half-ass love, from anyone. Aubs, *you* went into that shit with *your* eyes wide open. I offered *you* a position on my team where I could have helped *you* but *you* turned it down. Everything that *you* don't want to watch is on *you*. Stop whining about it and take some accountability for what's happening, and not happening. in your own life. It can't all be on me." I gave her with tough love.

She stood up from the bed and brought her hand from behind her back. She had a gun with a silencer on it. A fucking silencer, where does one even find that, a Spy store or some shit? I slowly backed away from her.

"What are you doing?" were the only words that came to me mind. Cliché, I know.

"Saving a lot of people heartache from you."

"We are supposed to be friends." I reminded her, my voice quivering.

"Yes, we were supposed to be. Then I realized, a long time ago, you have no clue what that word even means."

Just then, it dawned on me. The calls and the brakes were her.

"It was you that tried to kill me," I blurted out.

"Yes. Then I realized that if I wanted to be sure it happened, I would have to do it myself. Face to face. People like you always weasel out of it any other way. Now, I can be the only one for Franklin and start to win myself. Instead of watching you get everything your damaged ass has always wanted." She said to me as she clicked the hammer back on the gun.

I knew there was no getting out of this. Not for her or for myself. At least I knew that the bedroom cameras would catch all of this. They were tucked behind a teddy bear on my dresser. They had a clear view of who killed me. I had been to my lawyer so I knew that my daughter would be cared for the rest of her life. Knowledge that gave me a bit of peace in this moment.

Closing my eyes, I thought of her pretty little face and said a prayer, it was the last thing I ever did.

# Epilogue

ALL THE PEOPLE from my life had been called together by my lawyer. It was for the reading of my will. Bucky and Leona were first. I was wrong for messing with her husband, that's true, but she had her own secrets. I knew that Bucky had some guilt over our relationship. When the lawyer handed him the envelope, he opened it.

In there he found pictures of Leona in a passionate embrace with his best friend. There were more pictures that showed them going into and coming out of various hotels. Now, he knew the truth. The look he gave her before he threw the pictures in her face and stormed out was priceless.

I had also written him a letter letting him know how much he meant to me. How much I appreciated him making me feel loved and safe. That one he had tucked in his pocket and read when he got in the car. With tears streaming, he pounded on the steering wheel before peeling off. I wish I could be there to comfort him. It just wasn't meant to be.

The next was for Hugh and Cheyenne. Again, there was a letter for his eyes only. I knew she didn't know that we had lost a life together. When that happened, it softened me toward her. I knew that the same had happened to her. My letter was one of apology and congratulations on their upcoming child. Hugh's letter told him that I wish I had been strong enough to leave the hurt behind and move on with him. It begged him to be good to Cheyenne and also to their child.

I had a friend that used the same make-up artist. It's how I found out she was pregnant before he even knew. The letter given to him by my lawyer was the first he heard of it. He turned to her and asked her if it was true. She nodded her head yes and took his hand and placed it on her stomach. He kissed her, helped her to stand and they walked out hand in hand. The best I could hope for him was happiness. It was how much I loved him. Even though I was always afraid to let him in completely.

The next was for my Franklin. I left him fifty thousand to go towards his start-up. He was brilliant and I believed in him. He hugged Aubrey and cried still not knowing that he was hugging my killer. He would know in about ten minutes.

Taylor was there, sulking. She was always in some foul mood. I know she thought she would get the full business if I died, but that wasn't the case. My lawyer let her know that she could keep her clients but she had a new partner, my daughter. For the time being, her interest would be seen over by my assistant. I had taught her everything and she was a far better stylist than Taylor ever could be. In three years, when my daughter was eighteen and enrolled in fashion school, she and my assistant would work side by side, knowing that my daughter was the boss.

This surprised everyone. No one knew that I even had a daughter, except my mother and Franklin. Let alone that I was in touch with her. I requested that she and her adoptive parents sit in the hall until everyone in there had received what I had prepared for them. Then she would be told what I had left for her.

Taylor was pissed. She stood up and stormed from the room going on about how she would rather leave with nothing than become the subordinate to a secretary and a child. Something told me she would change her mind. She hadn't been good with her money and needed to keep working. If she were smart, she would stay on, and work out her contract, which reverted to my assistant and daughter's names but remained valid upon my demise. Then, she could take her clientele with her. Maybe by then, they could have gained A-list actors and actresses like the ones I styled for.

My mother sat there in her fur with glasses on and Kleenex in her hand. She had let the pedophile move back in. She thought that I didn't know because I didn't speak on it. I knew she never loved me, so she wasn't about to profit from my death. Not only did she find out that my daughter was my heir, but she also found out that both houses now belonged to Latoya. She could buy them from my daughter at three hundred and fifty thousand dollars, each. Or, she and he could pack up and be out of there in sixty days.

I made sure to let her know that I was being kind in allowing any of it with everything that she had allowed to happen to me. The two months was so could find a job and so could he. They could go rent a little apartment somewhere if they couldn't get a loan for the house. Which, how could they when she hadn't worked in over ten years and he was a recent parolee?

Just watching the look on her face as she snatched the glasses off and begged my lawyer to check again and see if I had left her anything at all was making it a little easier for me to be gone. She should have known that one day, she would get what she deserved, which was jack shit from me. My grandmother had begged me to help her out before she died. I think I did more than my share. Now, she could see what it was like to work for what you need and want. The way I had to.

She also stormed out, tears streaming. Hopefully, she would sell that fur and some other things in the house to help her out. I hope she had been saving the money I gave her every month. If not, skid row, here she comes.

Next, was the surprise for Aubrey. My lawyer asked to be excused for a moment and for Aubrey and Franklin to stay. When he returned, he had the two detectives that were working my case with him. They walked over to Aubrey and placed her under arrest for my murder.

Franklin stood to defend her until they told him that once the phone calls had started and an attempt had been made on my life, I had cameras installed. I instructed my lawyer to let the police know this and where they were located in case anything, untoward, happened to me. Once they both heard about the cameras in my bedroom, which is where I was found after Franklin called the police when he hadn't heard from me in two days, she hung her head and began to cry.

He backed away from her in shock. "How could you? Tell me they're wrong, Brey. Tell me."

"I think I need a lawyer." These were the only words she uttered as she was handcuffed and taken out. She took a plea to spare my daughter a trial. She would do thirty years with no chance for parole until she had served twenty-five years.

That was fine with me. Her best years would be behind her, plus, I knew her. She would never last in prison anyway. Once she was hauled off and Franklin followed behind, in shock, my daughter was called in along with her adoptive parents.

The lawyer let them know that Latoya was now worth over seven million dollars and it was only increasing. The business was in her name and the clothing line would still have her designs and input. Even though she was only fifteen, it was all in her name.

I had assembled a team for her that I did trust. Her parents would receive a stipend each month for her living expenses. Once she finished fashion school, with her minor in business, she would be twenty-two and take over everything. When she turned twenty-five, her complete trust would be handed over to her. I also left her a letter telling her how much I loved her.

I told her to not be bitter. It only held you back from greatness and love. It let her know that everything I did and endured, I did so that she wouldn't have to. That I knew she would make me proud. I let her know, even though I wasn't here in the physical form, I would be around her all the time, wrapping her in my love. She was the best and purest part of me. She was my pride, joy, and reason that I kept my sanity. Last, but not least, we would forever be, Latoya and Reese.

What she didn't know is that she would receive a letter on every birthday from me. I had sat down and written them up until the day she was married and birthed her children. Letting her know that I will always be there.

Her envelope was full of pictures of her that she didn't know I had taken. Pictures of her sleeping on the plane. Ones with her enjoying fashion week. Her working hard on sketches and even diving into a pool when we visited the world's largest waterpark. I always wanted her to know that I saw her, that I loved her, no matter how horribly things had ended.

She was not to be bitter or angry but to remember me in a good light. This she had to do, because she may be the only one that would.

---

Question for prizes: Did Reese deserve to die? Why or Why not? The top two answers sent to
DREAMWAKEWORKPUBLISHING@Gmail.com will receive a gift card. Think hard! And, as
always, thank you for the support. Leave a Review!

The End

Find other works by National Best-Selling Author **ASEERA** on
Amazon and Goodreads
Dreamwakework.com

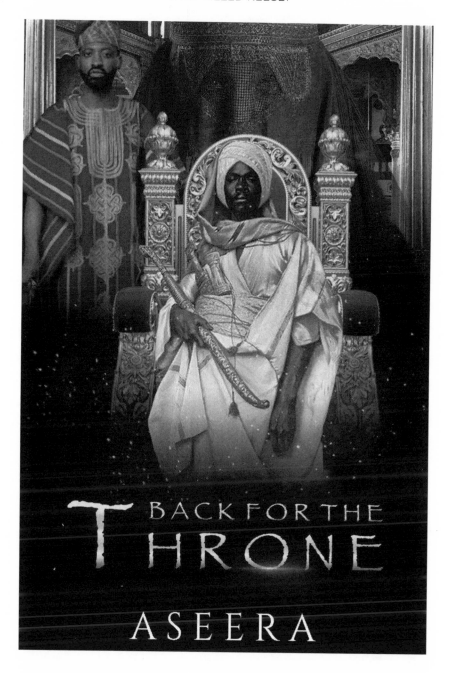

Made in the USA
Middletown, DE
27 August 2023

37446557R00038